Herbert

PROFESSOR WATERMELON

ILLUSTRATED BY JOSH SMART

Jake !
Beeeelieve in Yourself !!...

Professor Watermelon

DEDICATION

For Aunt Sherry – P.W.

For Bryiah and Layni – J.S.

Chapter 1

The Moldy Banana Peel

On the outskirts of Hogsville was a dump, and in that dump was a heap of trash. Nestled in that heap of trash was a moldy banana peel, and in that moldy banana peel lived a family of flies. It was dinnertime.

"Pass the rotten eggs," hollered Otis.

"More chunky milk!" Buford belched.

"Excuse you!" said their mother.

"Boys will be boys," said their father, belching himself.

Herbert, the youngest, sat quietly raking his slop from one side of his plate to the other.

"Eat, boy!" said his father.

"I'm not hungry," said Herbert.

"Darling, you must eat," said his mother.

"Herbert doesn't like our food," said Otis, his mouth full of rotten bologna.

"Herbert likes things nice and neat and everything sweet," said Buford, between belches. "I caught him on a honeysuckle this morning."

"You WHAT!" Herbert's father slammed his fists to the table, rattling the plates. "HERBERT!"

Herbert lowered his head.

"No son of mine will be caught slurping nectar," yelled his father. "You might as well be a BEE!"

"The Queen Bee," said Otis, chuckling.

The Queen Bee, Herbert thought. If only I was eating at her table.

Herbert's mother pushed her plate away and crossed her hands. "Darling, don't you like anything I fix?"

Herbert sank further into his chair. "May I be excused?"

"No!" said his father. "You will sit here until you clean that plate."

There was no way Herbert could follow those orders. He would much rather die than eat garbage. Yes, he loved the sweet nectar of honeysuckles, the velvety cream of buttercups, and the irresistible sunflower pollen. He was different. He couldn't fool anybody.

So, Herbert just sat there staring at his food. Everyone else finished their dinners. His father and brothers went outside to play a quick game of flyball before sundown, while his mother stacked the dirty plates in the cupboard and collected the scraps in a bowl for a future casserole.

"Now, I can't keep doing this, Herbert," his mother told him, clearing his plate and excusing him from the table. "Your father is going to find out and be angry at both of us."

"I'm sorry, mother," Herbert said. "I'm sure you're a great cook. I just can't eat slop."

Herbert's mother nodded and handed him a small bowl of honeysuckle nectar she had hidden under the kitchen sink. "I know, Darling. Now take this and slurp it in your bedroom."

"Thank you, mother," said Herbert.

She nodded kindly. Herbert buzzed upstairs to his room.

"And for flying out loud, don't let your father find out," his mother called after him.

Chapter 2

Slop! Slop! Slop!

When Herbert woke the next morning, he ironed his white collared shirt, his brown and yellow-checkered pants and his green argyle socks. After putting those on, he slipped into a baby blue cashmere sweater vest. Herbert was a master at finding junkyard gems, especially when it came to his own apparel. He could spend hours collecting snippets of cloth to sew into his one-of-a kind fashions.

After dressing, Herbert headed downstairs, knowing for certain he would catch more grief over breakfast. He would try slipping out of the house as quickly as he could.

"Good morning, Herbert," said his mother as he buzzed into the kitchen.

"Sit down and eat, son," said his father. "Rancid bacon, fresh from the trash truck."

Buford and Otis were already facedown into their plates, wolfing up their morning slop.

"I have a bit of a stomach ache," Herbert said, wincing at the rotten meat.

"If you'd eat a decent meal once in a while…" His father began ranting, but his words turned into loud grunts from overstuffing his mouth.

Herbert grabbed his satchel and headed for the door. The stench was more than he could bear, worse than fried rotten bologna.

"I don't know where you hang out all day, Herbert, but I know it's not with your brothers," hollered his father. "If you don't bring home your share of slop today, you're grounded."

Slop. Slop. Slop. Herbert was sick of slop. Yes, he understood that slop is what all flies live for, except for him. Yet his father sent him and his brothers to rummage the dump for slop everyday. Herbert wanted to tell his father to collect his own slop, but his father had gained a lot of weight and couldn't fly long distances, or so he said. He seemed to have no trouble playing flyball with Herbert's brothers.

"And please don't go beyond the dump, Herbert," insisted his mother. "Dragonflies are bad this year, worse than frogs."

"I'll be fine," said Herbert, although he was scared to death of dragonflies. These monsters lived near Fly Swatter Creek and were known to venture to the edge of the dump sometimes. They were also known to eat flies alive, one limb at a time. Just the thought made Herbert quiver.

"Sure you don't want to wait for your brothers?" she asked.

"He's too slow," said Otis, sputtering chunks of rotten meat between words.

"Yeah, and he's afraid to get dirty," said Buford.

Herbert's father grumbled beneath his breath.

"I'll be back before sundown," said Herbert, fleeing through the front flap before anyone could say another word.

Herbert flew as fast as he could away from the moldy banana peel. He wanted to avoid any chance of his brothers catching up with him. They were notorious for pushing him around and playing humiliating jokes on him.

A few weeks ago they had trapped him inside a tuna can. Herbert hadn't found his share of slop, so Otis had said, "No problem. We saved you some inside that can over there." Herbert should have known better. No sooner had he gotten inside the can, his brothers pounced on the lid, squeezing it shut. The can was full of slop all right – full of hot rotten tuna. If there was one thing that Herbert hated, it was the smell of tuna. But hot rotten tuna caused him to faint, and he did. Herbert's brothers thought they had killed him, so they dragged him out by his sweater vest, and when Herbert woke up, a fountain of barf spewed into his brothers' faces. If this was any other fly who had barfed on them, Buford and Otis would have lapped it up with pure joy, but Herbert's barf was regurgitated nectar. This was as appealing to Buford and Otis as the rotten tuna had been with Herbert. Both of his brothers heaved and gagged and returned the sickly favor right back into Herbert's face. This exchange of vomit repeated four or five times. From that incident forward, Otis and Buford had kept their distance from Herbert, but Herbert wasn't sure how long this freedom would last.

When the moldy banana peel was far from sight, Herbert slowed down. Rounding a heap of flattened tires, Hebert flew straight into a swarm of his brothers' friends.

"Look who it is," said their ringleader. He was shiny green, the type of fly that usually hangs out along highways waiting for road kill. "Sherbert, right?"

"Herbert! Herbert! Sherbert! Sherbert!" the rest of the swarm chanted. They were the same species as Herbert, the smaller gray type, but they still had no sympathy.

Used to being cornered, Herbert slipped right through the crowd and zipped away.

"Nice checkered pants, Orville Redenflyer!"

Herbert was good at tuning out insults, but he would be lying if he said they didn't hurt just a little. But he would be beyond that stinky old dump and those stinky old flies in a matter of seconds. His safe haven was just beyond Hogsville 101. There, Herbert could be himself, and no one could stop him.

Chapter 3

Herbert's Studio

Herbert looked all around before darting inside the hollow peach tree. The last thing he wanted was for someone to discover his secret peach orchard studio. His favorite things were kept there, including his honey recipe portfolio.

Herbert had spent countless hours decorating his studio with unearthed treasures from the dump. The floor was tiled in square mother of pearl beads from a broken necklace. The walls were delicately painted periwinkle blue from a discarded bucket of paint. In the center of the studio hung an ornate ruby chandelier. Herbert was sure it was some old human's unwanted costume jewelry, but who cared? It suited Herbert just fine. Throughout the studio were very fine pieces of furniture that Herbert had built with birch twigs. But Herbert's most prized possession was what hung above his roll top desk – a print of Her Majesty the Queen Bee. Herbert had carefully removed it from a honey jar and framed it in gold. Often times, he found himself in a daze, staring at the glossy portrait, imagining what it would be like to work for such perfection as Her Majesty.

Yes, Herbert dreamed of the day he could offer the queen a pail of his honey. Of course she would wonder how a fly had learned how to make such perfect sweetness, although Herbert wouldn't be able to answer. No one had taught him; he just always knew how. It was simply part of his brain, like knowing how to fly or knowing how to sneeze. What Herbert did know was that his honey tasted a trillion times better than the samples he had taken from discarded honey jars in the dump.

But he worried what the Queen and other bees would think of him if he visited the hive. He was a fly, after all, who had been born in a dump – not the type of place bees fancy much. As far as Herbert was concerned, that day would probably never come anyway. At least he had his studio, where he was safe and free of worries.

Herbert placed his satchel beside his birch twig chair and rolled back the top of his desk where he found his "to do" list written neatly on a square of old paper bag.

1. Taste batch #313 for quality control
2. Sing to batch #314
3. If there's time, gather more peach blossom nectar
4. BEWARE OF DRAGONFLIES!

Herbert's mother was right. Dragonflies were horrible this year. They were traveling further and further from the swamp, which was far far away. Herbert had only seen one dragonfly in his entire lifetime, which was plenty. The brute had dragged off one of his brothers' friends. Oh, it was a horrendous sight because everyone knew the poor fly's fate. He would be eaten limb by limb, then his body, then his head. AWFUL! He hoped he never encountered another one, and thinking about the infested swamp gave him nightmares.

Unfortunately, the swamp wasn't the only dangerous place for flies. Directly beyond the peach orchard was Fly Swatter Creek. There were bullfrogs the size of bowling balls hiding out along those banks. Herbert had nearly been tongue-slimed one day while

searching for wildflowers. To say the least, that was his last visit to
Fly Swatter Creek.

After folding his "to do" list, Herbert placed it in the top pocket
of his sweater vest along with his charcoal pencil. He then knelt
down and opened a secret door in the wall below the desk, leading
him to his honeycomb corridor.

"My eyes!" yelled a cranky voice. "Shut that darn door."

"Sorry, I thought you'd be asleep," said Herbert, closing the
door quickly behind him. The only light remaining was that which
came from the small cracks in the tree's inner wall. This was fine with
the old termite because her eyes had had time to adjust, but sudden
bursts of light sent her senses into overload.

"Stomach ache," said the old termite, popping her head out
from a hole. "I swear, if I have to bore another hole into this retched
tree, I'll just die."

Lucy had lived in the old peach tree longer than Herbert had
been alive. Her colony had taken over the tree ages ago, but she was
the only one left. She had told the story to Herbert before –
something about humans and a toxic spray – but Lucy would get
grumpy if Herbert asked too many questions. And that's pretty much
how their relationship worked except for the deal they had made. If
Lucy would bore the holes into the peach tree for Herbert's honey
production, Herbert would bring her morsels of exotic wood tossed
away in the dump. Balsa wood was her favorite. It was tender, tasty
and chewy; at least that's what Lucy said.

"Well, you've done an excellent job," said Herbert, pulling a
small morsel of Balsa wood from his pocket and handing it to the
termite. "I should be able to stock that honeycomb by the end of the
week."

"I don't care what you do with it," said Lucy. "I'm taking a
vacation."

"Where are you going?"

"My hole," she said, dragging the last syllable. Lucy inched away.
A sliver of light exposed her translucent skin, giving Herbert a
glimpse of her sagging and tired old face.

"Take as much time as you need," said Herbert.

"If I needed your permission, I would have asked for it," said
Lucy. "Now, keep it quiet."

Herbert moseyed down the corridor to batch #313. With one

hand, he pulled back the wax covering to a small compartment filled with honey. Dipping a finger into the gooey substance, Herbert pulled out a glob of honey and stuck it inside his mouth.

"Delicious," he squealed, clapping his hands together. "One more week and you should be ready to harvest."

Herbert had a habit of talking to the honey because he knew it listened. He had once found a magazine clipping from the dump titled, "Tomato Talk." It said that to grow prize-sized tomatoes, you must talk to your tomato vines every day. Words of encouragement would not only grow larger tomatoes but sweeter ones too. After reading this information, Herbert flew straight to his honeycomb and began talking to his honey. Lo and behold, that batch of honey was the sweetest Herbert had ever tasted. But Herbert had not stopped there. He began singing to his honey too, which produced outrageous results. Here is the song he sang:

> *Sweet sweet nectar oh so pure*
> *Collected from Mother Nature*
> *Give it a week and soon you'll be*
> *The sweetest most fabulous Honey*

Herbert buzzed down to batch #314 to sing it his special song. He sang this song to each batch of honey at least three times a day. But when he got there and right before he opened his mouth to sing the first word, the sound of breaking glass startled him. Herbert froze. The breaking and crashing sounds got louder, and it was coming from his studio.

Chapter 4

Ransacked

Herbert peeked through the door under his desk.

"We know you're in here, you little freak!" yelled the shiny green fly Herbert had sped away from earlier. "Show your face, twinkle-toes!"

In fact, the whole swarm of flies was packed into Herbert's studio, including his brothers.

"Herbert!" yelled Otis. "Wait till dad hears about this!"

"Yeah, you'll be grounded for the rest of your sissy life," said Buford. "No wonder you don't bring home any slop. You're too busy decorating."

Herbert could care less about what his dad or his brothers thought right now. He looked around his studio and saw that it had been ransacked. His furniture was busted to pieces. His cobalt vase lay shattered on the ground. Flies were taking turns swinging from his ruby chandelier. But what could Herbert do? He was clearly outnumbered, so he just watched his beloved studio get demolished as a plump tear gathered in his eye.

"What part of quiet don't you understand?" said a voice behind him.

Herbert looked at Lucy and put a finger to his mouth. Lucy inched toward the cracked door and took a squinted look just as the shiny green fly flew up and barfed on the Queen Bee.

Herbert slumped to the ground. Lucy punched her way through the door. Before Herbert could stop her, she was in the middle of the studio. "HALT!" she yelled from the top of her lungs.

Herbert squeaked but laid low.

"HALT! I say!"

"Well, well, well. What do we have here," said the shiny green fly, landing before the old termite. The rest of the flies assembled behind him.

"If you know what's best for you, you'll leave this instant," growled Lucy.

"But we just got started, you see," said the shiny green fly, rubbing his hands together. "Where's little Sherbert, anyway?"

"I said, LEAVE!"

"If we don't?" the shiny green fly said with a smirk.

Instantly, Lucy pulled back her lips, baring at least three rows of gleaming, razor-sharp teeth.

"Bring it!" she said.

"They're probably dentures," said Buford.

"Yeah, how old are you? A ba-zillion?" said Otis.

The others laughed, but the laughing stopped when Lucy picked up a busted chair leg and bit it in two with one simple bite.

"I'm outa here," said Otis.

"Me too," said Buford.

"What? You're gonna let this antique scare you away?" said the shiny green fly.

But when Lucy rushed towards them snapping her jaws, the room cleared.

"We'll be back, Sherbert!" the green fly sneered.

Once the flies cleared, Herbert stepped out into his studio. Lucy crawled back inside the honeycomb corridor, covering her eyes.

"Your place is trashed," she said. "I'd help you clean it up, but my eyes are killing me."

"Thank you," said Herbert. "For everything, but I don't think I'll be cleaning this mess either. By the sounds of it, they'll be back. It's no use."

Herbert surveyed the damage and hung his head. "What am I going to do?" he whispered.

"I don't know, kid," said Lucy, backing away into the darkness.

Herbert sat on the ground and listened to his thoughts. If he went home, his father would come unglued on him. He already knew that if he stayed put, the flies would be back to harass him and who knew what else, and if Herbert moved his studio to another tree, it would be a matter of time before they found that one, too. There was simply no hope. Why won't they just let me be, he wondered.

"That's it!" Herbert said out loud, looking up at the soiled picture of the Queen. "I'll be a bee!"

Chapter 5

To the Hive

Herbert packed his honey portfolio along with some other necessities in his satchel. Taking an empty pail back into the honeycomb corridor, he crept down to batch #312 and filled his pail with honey and secured the lid.

If there was one thing in life that Herbert was confident about, it was his honey. The queen would only have to take a tiny bite to realize his genius. She would undoubtedly ask him to join the hive right then and there. Hopefully.

Herbert tiptoed down to Lucy's hole to see if she was awake. He wanted to say goodbye, but as he approached her chambers her snores echoed down the corridor. Instead of waking her, Herbert pulled a piece of brown paper and a charcoal pencil from his satchel and wrote her a note:

Dear Lucy,

I've woken you enough in one day, so I decided to leave this note instead. I've left to try my luck at the beehive. Thanks for sticking up for me today!

Your friend,
Herbert

After folding the note, Herbert tucked it under one of Lucy's hands. He whispered goodbye, and headed for his ransacked studio.

Once there, he found a lid for his pail and surveyed his studio one last time. A deep pain thudded in his heart as he turned his back on his beloved haven and buzzed out of the hollow tree. Hiding behind some leaves, Herbert looked all around to make sure the swarm of flies was not preparing an ambush. Luckily, his way was clear, except for not knowing where the hive was.

Chapter 6

Fly Swatter Creek

While leaving the Orchard, Herbert thought about his mother back at the moldy banana peel. He felt awful for leaving without saying goodbye, but facing his father was out of the question. Certainly, his mother would understand. If there was anyone who understood him, it was her. She never made him feel less of fly for the things he did. Herbert loved his mother, and Herbert knew that she loved him back. He just hoped that she knew it wasn't her fault he was leaving.

Buzzing through the last row of peach trees, Herbert contemplated the obstacle before him. He had sworn he would never come back to this horrifying place, but there it was. Fly Swatter Creek.

Herbert fought the desire to turn around, but he knew the hive must be somewhere beyond the creek. All other directions would lead him into Hogsville, and no Queen in her right mind would settle her hive there. So, over the creek it was.

The air cooled, and Herbert could hear and smell the fresh water trickling over the rocks. And that's exactly where he needed to stay. Bullfrogs don't like the ripples. They hang out where the water is still and murky so they can hear the buzzing of a fly's wings and snatch the unfortunate soul from the sky.

But flies weren't the only beasts Herbert had to be watchful of. If he flew too high, a chickadee might snag him. And he had to be on the lookout for dragonflies, no matter how high or low he flew.

But this wasn't the time to think about ways to exit the world. Herbert needed to focus if he was going to make it to the other side. Clenching his fist onto the pail of honey, Herbert darted from rock to rock.

So far, so good. No frogs. Dodging more rocks, Herbert felt that he was getting the hang of it, when out of nowhere leapt a giant trout with its mouth wide open.

"Holy SHARK!" Herbert screamed, barely dodging the giant fish's cavernous throat. Zipping between two rocks, Herbert landed to catch his breath. Why hadn't anybody warned him of sharks, he wondered.

"Those are trout," said a low husky voice.

Herbert slowly swiveled his head to meet the luminous yellow eyes of a hefty bullfrog.

Herbert tried to scream but there was nothing there. His body trembled, shaking loose the honey pail in his hand.

In a blink of an eye, the bullfrog unleashed his tongue and…

Chapter 7

A Rock and a Hard Place

The bullfrog reeled in Herbert's pail.

"Calm down, brotha," said the frog, giving back Herbert his honey. "I ain't gonna eat you."

"But uh…why not?" Herbert stumbled.

"No offense, but I'm vegan," said the frog.

"Pleasure to meet you, Vegan. I'm Herbert." Herbert extended his hand apprehensively.

"No, no, no. The name's Norm, and so happens I'm Vegan."

"Sorry, Norm, but I'm confused," said Herbert, shaking the frog's pointer finger.

"Vegans don't eat meat, and you so happens to fall in that category."

"Lucky me."

"That's right!" the frog laughed, slapping his tongue up against a rock, peeling off a chunk of moss. Instantly the moss was in the frog's mouth being chewed like cud. This bullfrog really lived up to his name.

"Where you goin' anyways?" said Norm. "Ain't nothing dead around here to lay eggs on."

"First of all, I don't lay eggs," said Herbert. "And secondly, I don't go anywhere near rotting carcasses."

"Excuuuuuse me," said Norm.

"Sorry, I've had a bad day, but it's looking up. I've run into a vegan frog that's not going to eat me."

"Rather eat poop!" said Norm, chuckling.

"Good, although I know some flies that go crazy over the stuff. Ick!" said Herbert. "But to answer your question, I'm headed for the beehive."

"But why?"

"To make honey."

Norm nearly lost his meal, he laughed so hard. "You're kiddn', right?"

"Coming from a frog that doesn't eat flies - you have no room to talk."

"Suppose you've got a point," said Norm, holding out a fist. "Cheers to the oddballs!"

"Cheers," said Herbert touching his fist to Norm's.

"So, I'm bet'n you need across this crick?"

"Yep."

"Only one safe way to get there."

"How?"

"Inside my mouth."

"You're out of your mind," said Herbert, backing away.

"Son, you just saw me eat a wad of moss, and if I wanted to eat you, I would've done so by now."

Herbert pondered the frogs reasoning, and Norm was right. He had had several opportunities to snag Herbert for a meal. And Herbert certainly didn't want to be swallowed by a trout, and by the looks of it, Fly Swatter Creek was as populated with fish as it was frogs.

"Fine," said Herbert. "But if you eat me, I'll come back from the dead and haunt you till you find a waterfall to hop off of."

"Quit your yapp'n and get to snapp'n."

"How do I get in?"

"You want the easy or the hard way?"

"Easy, I guess…"

In a split second, Norm had slung out his tongue, retrieving Herbert, honey and all, and sat him inside his right cheek. In the process, a drop or two of Herbert's honey dripped onto Norm's tongue.

"On second thought," said Norm. "You sweet for a fly."

"Don't get any ideas," said Herbert. "You're tasting my honey."

"Honey," said Norm. "That's the sweetest taste that's made it inside my mouth."

"Thank you," said Herbert.

"You sure you ain't a bee?"

Herbert laughed, and held tight. For being inside of a frog's mouth, Herbert was quite comfortable. To his surprise it wasn't sticky or slimy at all. In fact, he had never sat on a cushier surface in his life – not even the petal of a buttercup could compare. There was a lingering scent of damp moss and algae, but that was fine. Herbert just sat back and relaxed until Norm launched from the ground.

Chapter 8

The Other Side

"I think I'm going to puke," said Herbert, once they got to the other side and Norm opened his mouth.

As fast as Norm had sat Herbert inside his cheek, he was just as quick to sit him on the bank.

"Ain't nobody chuckin in my mouth," said Norm.

"I'm fine now," said Herbert, brushing off his checkered pants.

"You sure do have style for fly, now that I got a good look at you."

"The only perk of living in the dump – every blue moon you might unearth a treasure."

"If I didn't spend half my time in the water, I might dig a pair of those drawers."

"Yeah, but you might have to add some fabric in the leg department."

"I'm glad I met you, little fly," said Norm with a wide smile. "Just holler my name if you need back across this crick."

"Likewise," said Herbert. "And I hope I can pay you back someday."

"No need, brotha," said Norm. "It's just good to have a friend."

Herbert smiled and nodded, while grabbing his pail of honey. He had turned to leave when he remembered something.

"Do you happen to know which way to the bee hive?" asked Herbert.

Norm had already leapt off the bank, but before he dove into the water he called back, "Just beyond the Swamp."

"The swamp?" said Herbert slowly.

The reality hit him like a ton of flat tires. Once again, Herbert's mind was filled with images of beastly dragonflies devouring little guys like him. Hoping for Norm to poke his head out of the water, Herbert waited to get some more information, but Norm was gone.

Herbert was mad at himself. Why hadn't he thought this through before leaving his studio? He didn't know how he would find his way to the hive. Maybe he would ask peaceful acquaintances or follow a bee, but what Herbert hadn't planned for was the swamp.

Just then an idea fired off in his mind. If he would have taken time to think of every scenario of his future, he would've probably never left, and that was not an option. Herbert decided then and there that he would face whatever fears unfolded in his way. He would make it to that hive one way or another. Unfortunately, he still hadn't a clue how to get there.

After careful consideration, Herbert decided to take the route that would get him farthest from the dump. That is certainly where he would build a hive – as far away from the stench, mold, and rot as he could get. That meant he must fly through the thick forest ahead of him.

Herbert grabbed his honey, tightened the satchel on his back, and buzzed off. A few minutes into the forest, he found it darker and spookier than he had imagined, but he kept going in spite of the eeriness.

Whizzing around gigantic fir trees twenty times the size of the peach trees he was used too, Herbert gained speed. He didn't know how long the forest would last, but he hoped to get through it before dark.

He didn't.

The moon traded places with the sun, while creepy shadows darted through the trees.

"Whoo who whoo who whoolll…"

Herbert had never heard that sound before.

"WHOO WHO WHOO WHO WHOLLL!!!"

A monstrous bird swooped over him, sending him somersaulting through the air. Gripping his honey, Herbert crashed into a plume of ferns. He lay there stunned for a few moments before brushing himself off and checking for cuts and bruises. Then, he saw the huge bird hover back to a tree branch. It had something twitching and squirming in its mouth.

"A screech owl," Herbert whispered.

He had read about these birds in a discarded biology textbook. They eat mice and other small, helpless creatures in the forest, and they have excellent eyesight. Herbert ducked underneath a frond to keep safe and decided he was staying put that night.

Herbert looked around for a small twig, some dry leaves, and a rock. He had read that if he spun the bottom of the twig against the rock and leaves, the friction would ignite the leaves. And since forest predators usually stay away from fire, Herbert was determined to make this work. Three hours and two calloused hands later, Herbert had his fire. He quickly shaped a teepee of larger sticks around the small flames and added more dry leaves. In a matter of moments, flames swirled around the sticks. The campfire Herbert had hoped for crackled and popped, brightening the area around him. Success!

Settling in, Herbert opened his honey pail for a snack. He dipped his finger into the gooey honey and pulled out a glistening amber glob of pure sweetness. Making sure not to eat too much, he placed the lid back on the pail. He had to keep plenty to offer the queen when he arrived at the hive.

Herbert pulled some moss from a nearby rock to make a bed. A few moments later, he was asleep. He didn't hear the slurping sounds coming from behind the ferns.

Chapter 9

The Slippery Noodles

Herbert was jolted awake by the sound of loud music. Eyes wide open, he discovered that three banana slugs had descended upon his campfire. Herbert jumped up and rubbed his eyes.

"Hey," he yelled, not knowing what else to say.

The slugs paid no attention but continued playing their twangy music: one plucking a banjo, another strumming a bass fiddle, and the last blowing a harmonica. Surprise aside, Herbert wondered how these creatures could even play instruments with no hands. That's when he noticed the stretched folds of skin pulled from their long bodies into what resembled fingers.

"Can I help you?" Herbert shouted.

The slugs sang louder.

Greasy slugs we three may be
We sing our tunes in harmony
Through the woods we weave and wind
Slimy trails we leave behind

Herbert decided he may as well listen to the awkward trio, but when a pair of spoons flew his direction he didn't know whether to duck or catch. Despite his poor flyball skills, Herbert caught them in midair.

Slippery Noodles from Waterloo
Have no banjo? Spoons will do.
Slap them right inside your thigh
A Kentucky beat for you and I

Although Herbert was shocked with the spectacle before him, and not to mention that he had just woken up, he knew that slugs are harmless. And believe it or not, this was not the first time Herbert had had the opportunity to play the spoons. He knew exactly what to do, but instead of using his knee, Herbert used his hands. With one hand he held both spoons with the bowl sides back to back. Leaving a small space between the spoons, Herbert clapped them in the palm of his other hand, producing the Kentucky Bluegrass beat. Herbert followed the slugs' rhythm as they continued to sing. He was wide-awake now.

Picks up quick for a fly
Never met quite a guy
Hats are off to this lad
Makes us slugs mighty glad

With that, the song was over, except for the lingering harmonica.

"Name's Applejack," said the banjo player. He was yellow, long and thin.

"Mine's Tugg," said the bass fiddle player. He was yellow, short and stubby with black spots.

"And I'm JoBill," said the Harmonica player, taking a breath. He was yellow, short and stubby with no spots.

"My name is Herbert," said Herbert. "You sure make a loud wake-up call."

"Followed the light, is all," said Applejack. "But can't stay too long or we'll dry out by this fire."

"You play great music," said Herbert. "Where are you from?"

"We're the Slippery Noodles from Waterloo," said Tugg. "Just traveling through."

The harmonica player still hadn't stopped.

"Where's Waterloo?" said Herbert.

"Who knows," said Applejack. "By the way, where'd you learn to play the spoons like that?"

"From a book on Bluegrass music," said Herbert.

"Not too many flies know Bluegrass," said Tugg.

"As far as I know," said Herbert. "not many slugs know either."

"By golly, Applejack, the fly's got a point."

"Sure does!" said Applejack.

"We're stars!" said JoBill, taking another breath.

"Grand Ol' Opry! Here we come!" yelled Applejack.

"Slime! JoBill, slime!" hollered Tugg. "You're drying out."

The harmonica left Jobill's mouth. A few grunts later, he was enveloped in a glistening slime ball. Although Herbert was completely grossed out, he was also intrigued.

"How did he do that?" asked Herbert.

"That's like asking a dog how he barks," said Tugg. "He just does."

Herbert wondered if he could grunt and cause slime to erupt out of somewhere, but he quickly dismissed the thought.

"So, why are you out in the middle of the woods alone," said Applejack, stretching his eyeballs toward Herbert.

"I'm moving to the hive," said Herbert.

"You talking bees?" said Applejack.

"Yep," said Herbert, holding up his pail. "Hopefully the Queen accepts the honey I've made and offers me a position."

"At the Honeycomb Palace?" said Tugg. "We slid past there a month or so ago."

"Really!" Herbert's eyes gleamed. "You know how to get there?"

"Not very far at all," said Applejack.

"For a fly that is," added Tugg. "Just on the other side of the swamp inside the clover field."

"Once you get that far," said Applejack. "Just look for the giant sycamore tree in the middle. You can't miss it."

"Did you see any dragonflies?" said Herbert

"Hundreds," said Tugg. "But they don't bother us."

Herbert's stomach knotted. "They'll eat me."

"I don't know what to tell ya, buddy," said Applejack.

A wave of brilliance swept over Herbert. "I know," he said. "I'll cross the swamp at night while they're all sleeping! Why didn't I think of that before?"

"And he's smart too," said Tugg.

Herbert jumped up and down. "I can't thank you enough," he said.

"No problem kid," said Tugg. "But we better hit the trail before this fire takes its toll."

Herbert glanced at JoBill. His slime was quickly evaporating.

"Nice to know you," said Applejack.

"The pleasure is all mine," said Herbert.

The Slippery Noodles struck a chord and paraded into the night.

Herbert sat down by the fire and thought about the odd slug trio headed for the Grand Ole Opry. He thought about Norm, the vegan frog, back at Fly Swatter Creek. Maybe life wasn't so black and white outside the dump. The hairs on Herbert's arms tingled at the roots as his heart filled with hope. His chances at the hive seemed brighter and brighter. More now than ever, Herbert felt he had made the right decision to leave the moldy banana peel and his life at the dump behind, although he did miss his mother terribly.

As Hebert nestled by the fire to fall asleep, he once again realized he had forgotten to get directions to the swamp, and there was no way he was going to follow the slugs into the darkness. Hard telling what would be waiting out there to eat him.

Chapter 10

Something Left Behind

Herbert woke with the sun, although he could barely see it through the dense fir trees. Trying not to feel discouraged, he looked all around for a clue to which way he should proceed. He wanted to kick himself for missing the opportunity to get directions from the slugs, but when Herbert caught the reflection of the sun off of the sticky residue on the forest floor, he nearly leapt out of his checkered pants.

"SLIMY TRAILS!" Herbert shouted, echoing throughout the forest.

Herbert couldn't have asked for better directions. The path to the beehive was laid out right before him. He would have kissed the slugs if they were still around. Well, maybe not.

Throwing his satchel over his shoulder and grabbing his honey pail, Herbert dashed away, keeping the glistening trail in sight. He wove around the enormous tree trunks and over bundles of ferns and moss until he hit an invisible wall.

This is strange, Herbert thought right before panic ran cold through his veins. And when he noticed the sticky strands of silk stuck to his body, Herbert let out the most horrified shriek. Shaking and trembling, he tried getting loose, but the more he fought, the more stuck he got.

In a nanosecond Herbert was pinned beneath eight spindly legs.

"A fly!" said the spider. She was black with a big butt, sporting a striking red dot where the silk comes out. "But a flashy fly, I must say."

Herbert squirmed and lost his grip on the honey pail. It fell into a plume of ferns below.

"No need to fret," hissed the spider. "I'm not going to eat you yet. A dashing fly like yourself must be savored for a midnight snack."

"Please let me go," Herbert pleaded.

"And you smell so sweet," said the spider.

Oozing a thick strand of silk from her spinnerets, the spider spun Herbert into a tight ball. Herbert tried to scream, but his mouth was wrapped shut. Only muffled whimpers escaped through the silk.

"Silly fly, nobody can hear you," snickered the spider.

Certain he was going to die, Herbert was overwhelmed with horrid thoughts. He couldn't bare thinking of those fangs piercing his body. Of course Herbert knew that it would only sting for a little while. He had read that a Black Widow's venom paralyzes its victim. What a horrible way to die.

"You just hang tight, my sweet," said the spider. "I'll be visiting again tonight."

The spider climbed to the edge of her web and hid herself beneath a leaf, leaving Herbert to ponder his fate.

Reality flung itself directly into Herbert's heart. He realized then and there that he would never see his mother again – or any of his family for that matter. But Herbert mostly worried about his mother. She would never know what had become of him. More than anything, Herbert wished he had told his mother where he was going. He knew that she wouldn't be able to save him from this predicament, but at least she would have thought he was someplace that made him happy – the beehive.

The day lingered forever, proving to be the longest day Herbert had ever lived. He was going to die in a matter of hours, and there was nothing he could do about it. The more he tried to wiggle, the tighter the silk squeezed around his body.

Finally, the moon crept into the sky, reminding Herbert that midnight was only moments away. Herbert hoped for a miracle, but when he felt the vibrations of the web as the spider made her descent, he knew miracles were out of the question.

"Midnight," said the spider, climbing over Herbert. "Time to dine."

This was it. Everything was over. Herbert would never meet the Queen. He would never again make honey. He would never again do anything.

Herbert stared at the moon as the spider lowered her fangs.

"So sweet and tender," said the spider, pressing Herbert with one of her feet. "I'm in for a tasty treat."

Just as the spider's fangs touched Herbert's abdomen, something flew across the moon like a quick eclipse.

The spider raised her head. "NO!" she wailed. "STOP!"

In the blink of an eye, a gigantic Luna Moth swooped into the web, beating its humongous wings frantically. The spider darted towards the Luna Moth, baring her fangs, but with one flap of a wing, the spider was tossed from her own web. Herbert heard her high-pitched wails all the way to the ground - then a small thud.

Herbert felt a rush of relief, although he was still bound by silk. Luckily, the web had busted all around him, leaving his silk-ball dangling from a single thread. But soon the Luna Moth flapped its wings wildly one more time, setting itself and Herbert free.

Herbert fell to the ground, landing next to his honey pail in the plume of ferns. The silk ball provided cushion and the fall loosened the tight weave, allowing Herbert's hands and fingers room to move. One by one, Herbert snapped strands of silk until he was able to crawl out.

"I'm FREE!" he yelled.

Then Herbert remembered that the spider had fallen close by. Not knowing if she was dead or alive, Herbert took no chances. He grabbed his honey pail and buzzed off into the moonlit forest. Owls or no owls, spiders or no spiders, Herbert was not stopping. He was determined to flee the forest alive.

Flying low to the ground, Herbert followed the slug's trail, which shone in the moonlight. His body still ached from being bound so tightly, but he flew as fast as he could. He didn't even notice when the trail disappeared and was replaced with swampy water.

Chapter 11

The Swamp

If it hadn't been midnight and prime slumbering hour for the ferocious beasts dotting the lily pads below, Herbert would have quickly found himself in one of the dragonfly's jaws of death. And as hard it was not to let the horrifying stories he had grown up hearing cause him to buckle and faint, Herbert kept flying. Every now and then, he would let his gaze drift down to the dragonfly's protruding eyes, but with a quick snap of his head, Herbert would focus forward again.

The swamp smelled like Herbert's father's farts, which made Herbert gag. Covering his nose with one hand, he had no choice but to fly higher to get away from the stagnant water.

From this higher altitude, Herbert could see the outline of cattails bordering the swamp's edge. If the slugs were right, the beehive was just beyond those cattails in a clover field.

Clover, clover, clover, Herbert repeated to himself – anything to keep his mind from drifting to the danger lurking beneath him. Clover, clover, clover.

Time ticked slowly, but Herbert finally smelled the sweet clover instead of stagnant swamp water. His heart raced, but he knew he wasn't beyond the reach of danger's grip.

Mustering every last bit of energy in his body, Herbert coursed ahead. When the dark shadows began darting around him, Herbert was caught off guard. Just when he thought his only threat lay beneath him, a BAT snatched him from above.

This wasn't the first mouth Herbert had found himself inside, but unlike the vegan frog, this creature wanted to eat him. To the contrary, Herbert planned to make it to the beehive. Being swallowed was NOT part of the plan.

Herbert latched onto the bat's scratchy tongue like a leech to a water buffalo. With the hand that held the honey pail, Herbert began swinging. The honey pail ricocheted from one side of the bat's mouth to the other.

Herbert could feel the bat swooping up and down repeatedly, obviously trying to dislodge him from its tongue. Herbert held on tighter and swung harder, but the smell of bat saliva was about to make him puke. It smelled like the rotten leftovers in a cat food can.

Round and around, Herbert swung his pail, and just before his arms went completely numb, the bat must have realized it had bitten off more that it could chew

The bat hocked Herbert like a loogie into the starry sky. Flap-flapping away, squeaking and squawking like a disobedient dog running for the doghouse, the bat disappeared. Luck was certainly on Herbert's side, but he couldn't help but wonder how long that would last.

Surprisingly though, Herbert noticed the swamp was no longer beneath him. Instead, the heavenly scent of clover wafted from the ground. He had finally made it to the clover field. And even more thrilling was what loomed in the distance - a gigantic sycamore tree silhouetted by the moon.

Herbert could hardly contain himself. His dream was about to come true. Gazing at the sycamore tree, Herbert flew straight toward it. He was ready. The moment he had been waiting for was mere seconds away.

But Herbert felt a little ignorant when he approached the entrance of the imperial tree and found the hive asleep. Herbert had been so excited that he forgot what time it was. It was well past midnight, and only the soft buzz from the sleeping bees echoed though the hollow chambers.

Oh well, Herbert thought. I'll just camp out here next to this root.

Herbert landed on one of the sycamore's massive roots, took off his satchel, and put down the honey pail. He grabbed some dry grass and made a small nest. He nestled himself around until he was completely comfortable and then stared at the moon.

How wonderfully his life was about to change - Herbert was confident that the queen would instantly appraise his talents and offer him a job. Maybe he could be a taste-tester, a flower scout, or even a recipe writer.

As Herbert wound down with a mind full of happy thoughts, he drifted off to sleep. The long and treacherous journey was over.

He was awakened at sunrise with the tip of a spear to his neck.

Chapter 12

Long Live the Queen

"Should we spear him, Beauregard?" said one of the two guards.

"I don't know, Octavious," said the other. "The Queen hates a mess."

"Like her large butt could make it out the palace door," said the one who called himself Octavious, pushing the spear even closer to Herbert's neck.

"How dare you speak of the Queen like that," said Herbert.

The two guards were taken by surprise.

"WHAT?" they said together.

"You heard me," said Herbert, slapping the spear away from his neck.

"Not so fast … fly!" said the one who called himself Beauregard.

Herbert didn't know where this bravery was coming from. The drones were definitely bigger than him and for that matter, armed. But what he really couldn't understand was the guards' blatant insults to Her Majesty the Queen.

"I seek company with the Queen," Herbert declared.

"I beg your pardon," said Octavious.

Beauregard laughed out loud. "He seeks company with the Queen!"

"For what?" said Octavious.

Not knowing if he should tell the truth, since he didn't know where the truth would get him, Herbert paused and then told the truth anyway.

"I want to make honey," said Herbert proudly.

The two guards completely lost control and doubled over with gut-busting laughter.

"Honey," they laughed. "This fruit fly wants to make honey!"

"I'm not a fruit fly," Herbert said, irritated.

Octavious stopped laughing. "I don't know whether to laugh or be offended."

"Neither," said Herbert glaring at the guards.

"Let's take him in," said Beauregard. "I want to see the Queen's face when she hears this."

Octavious agreed with a sarcastic grin, and they both grabbed one of Herbert's arms and flew him inside.

Herbert was marveled at the rows and rows of honeycomb. And the sweet scent of beeswax and honey blossomed all around him. If he wasn't held captive by the guards, Herbert would have thought he had made it to heaven, although he was still confident the Queen would love his honey. His HONEY –

"We've got to go back," said Herbert. "I forgot my honey pail."

"Aw, he brought Her Majesty some honey," said Beauregard.

"I'm afraid you're not going to need it," said Octvious.

"Let me go!" Herbert struggled to get loose, but he was unsuccessful. The guards flew him to the Queen's chamber at the tip-top of the hive.

When Herbert caught his first glimpse of her, he broke out in a sweat. She was everything he thought she would be – regal, beautiful and … BIG. The guards planted Herbert before Her Majesty the Queen and giggled as they bowed and took several steps back, leaving Herbert standing alone.

"What business do you have here?" said the Queen with a puzzled stare.

"Hel – Hello Your Majesty." Herbert barely managed to squeeze the words from his mouth. "I've come to make honey."

"If this is some kind of joke, make yourself clear now," said the Queen, glancing at the guards.

"Not at all," said Herbert. "It has been my dream to live at the hive."

"Nonsense. You – are a fly!"

"I can assure you, I'm no ordinary fly, Your Majesty," said Herbert.

"That much is clear," said the Queen. "You've got quite the nerve to bother me with such a silly idea."

"But…"

"I've heard enough," said the Queen.

"If you would just…"

"I said enough," said the Queen. "Now please excuse yourself before you contaminate something."

"I was just-"

"GO!"

Herbert hung his head and turned around. From the corner of his eyes, he could see the guards snickering with delight. Before they had the chance to follow him, Herbert flew from the Queen's chamber and past the thousands of busy worker bees. Many of them stopped and stared at Herbert on his way out.

"Who's that?"

"Nasty fly!"

"Gross."

"He had the nerve to speak to Her Majesty?"

"Whatever for?"

"Idiot."

These were just some of the remarks Herbert overheard on his way out of the Sycamore tree. Even worse, Herbert felt the bees were right. Seriously, what business did he have at the hive? He wasn't a bee! He was a fly. What a silly notion to think he even had a chance? He was born in a dump for flying-out-loud!

Herbert flew from the hive and found his satchel and honey pail where he had left it. He put the satchel on his back but left the honey pail in the grass. It had been beaten up and half emptied already, and since there was ample clover around, Herbert would have plenty of food – although eating was the last thing on Herbert wanted to do. His desire was to get as far away from the hive as possible. It took everything he had not to burst into tears, but Herbert sucked it up and buzzed off, having no idea where he was headed or what he would do when he got there.

"Wait!" yelled a voice from behind him.

Herbert kept going, thinking the voice was coming from his own conscience.

"You forgot something," the voice yelled again.

Herbert could tell this time that the voice was that of a female - definitely not his conscience. Even though he didn't want to, he turned around.

"I think this is yours," said the dainty bee, holding out Herbert's honey pail.

"Thanks, but no thanks," said Herbert.

"I heard everything, and I'm sorry you were turned away," said the bee. "She's a bit cranky when it comes to change, Her Majesty, that is."

"I've noticed," said Herbert.

"I'm Sandy, a flower scout," she said. "What's your name? You look very nice by the way."

"Herbert."

"Well, Herbert, do you want your pail?"

"Absolutely not," said Herbert, wrinkling his brow. "It only reminds me of what a failure I am."

"Don't be so rough on yourself," said Sandy. "Like I said, the Queen is stuck in her ways, and you don't appear disgustingly gross – I mean, you look very nice for a fly. If I were the Queen, I would've given you a chance."

"But you're not," said Herbert. "Thanks anyway, but I just want to be alone right now."

Herbert flew off.

"Where do you live?" Sandy called after him.

"Nowhere," Herbert called back. He hoped the little bee would not follow him. He was in no mood for company.

Flying far far away from the giant sycamore tree and the dump for that matter, Herbert slowed down and looked behind himself to make sure he was alone. He hoped he had not hurt the bee's feelings, but Herbert was simply too hurt to talk. After all, what was he going to do now? All of his hopes and dreams had been shattered, and he knew that only punishment and ridicule would greet him if he went back to the dump.

Herbert thought about his mother. Waves of sorrow and longing washed over him. Maybe his mother would know what to do, but that was a useless thought now. She probably thought he was dead, or that he'd left because he didn't love her anymore. Herbert wondered what she was doing at that very moment. She was probably setting the breakfast table for his brothers and father. Herbert couldn't believe it, but he kind of missed them too, although he knew his brothers and father were probably relieved to find that he had dropped off the face of the planet..

Herbert continued flying until he heard the trickling of water. Maybe it was a river with lots of frogs. Maybe he would just go sit on the bank, close his eyes and wait to be eaten.

Chapter 13

Down by the River

Herbert found himself next to a small river, although much wider than Fly Swatter Creek. He landed between two rocks and sat there staring into the sky. If he was in danger from a frog, dragonfly, or any other carnivorous beast – so what!

"What's with the long face?" said a hollow voice, coming from beneath the rock.

Great, Herbert thought. More company.

When the massive claw exposed itself, Herbert didn't even flinch.

"Take me," Herbert said, his hands hanging limply at his side. "Just make it quick."

"I beg your pardon?" said the crawdad, fully exposed now.

"Don't you want to eat me?" said Herbert. "Just start with my head."

"Sounds like somebody needs to toughen his shell."

"Looks like you have a pretty tough shell," Herbert said numbly.

The crawdad laughed. "It's a metaphor – a figure of speech."

"I realize that." Herbert's voice indicated no interest in this tough shelled stranger.

"So you have run away from home," said the crawdad.

"How did you know?"

"The other flies don't understand you. They think you're strange."

"Okay, this isn't funny."

"And you found the grass is just as brown on the other side."

"What are you, the Wizard of Oz or something?"

"Who?"

"A character in a book I read, never mind."

"Life is full of disappointments," said the crawdad. "You've got to get used to it."

"I've spent my entire life trying to get used to it," Herbert said, standing straight and stomping a foot. "I want a better life, free of ridicule and harassment. I'm a fly that likes honey, SO WHAT! I don't deserve to be pushed around and called names."

"Honey, eh?" said the crawdad.

"I don't just like honey! I LOVE honey! And I can make it too – the best, most sweetest, most delectable tasting honey on the planet!"

"What's stopping you?"

Herbert slouched back onto the rock. "The Queen."

"So, you're giving up."

"Bingo."

"Nonsense!"

"I suppose you have a better alternative?" said Herbert, looking into the crawdad's beady eyes.

"Nope," said the crawdad.

"Great."

Herbert slid his back down the rock, landing his butt in the mud. If his outfit hadn't already been dirty, it was certainly dirty now. But Herbert didn't care what he looked like anymore. Why should he? He had no one to impress, and after all – he was just a disgusting fly.

"You're going to stay here until you figure it out," said the crawdad. "I'll fend off the frogs."

"Thanks," Herbert muttered. "But I'd rather one ate me."

The crawdad either ignored that last comment or didn't hear it. "But you're not leaving until you have a plan," he said.

"I have nowhere else to be, I guess."

Herbert didn't move for hours. He just stared at the rock ahead of him until his head hurt. Behind him he could hear the crawdad raking around in the mud. Herbert wondered why, but he couldn't muster the energy to look back to find out.

As the sun went down and the clouds slid over the moon, darkness settled over the river. The crawdad continued his scraping around in the mud, loud enough for Herbert to hear. This made him feel less alone and able to shut his eyes for some rest, but what he didn't expect was the sound of someone calling his name. And it wasn't the crawdad.

Chapter 14

Stranger in the Night

At first Herbert thought it was his mother, but the voice was too young. Herbert wondered if he should answer, but his decision was made for him.

"Over here!' yelled the crawdad.

When the source of the voice found him, Herbert was surprised to see it was Sandy, the little worker bee he had met earlier that day.

"I tasted your honey," she blurted. "It's heaven, simply divine!"

Herbert was thrown aback.

"Our hive doesn't even come close to producing such perfection," she continued. "You have to come back."

"How did you find me?" said Herbert.

"Your scent, of course," said Sandy, looking Herbert over. "Although you are exceptionally muddy, you're the sweetest smelling creature alive."

"That's comforting," said Herbert, standing a bit taller.

"So what do you say? Are you coming back or what?"

"Of course he will," said the crawdad, slipping himself into view.

Sandy screamed at the sight of the huge claw. Apparently she hadn't realized they had company.

"Easy, trigger," said the Crawdad, waving his claw. "This old thing is just for show. I eat dead fish, not bugs."

"Look," said Herbert. "I don't care how good my honey is. The Queen has already made her decision."

"But she hasn't tasted your honey," said Sandy, still eyeing the monstrous claw.

"And I doubt she will."

"That's where you are wrong," said Sandy. "One thing that matters the most to Her Majesty- -"

"Tradition?" Herbert interrupted.

"No, smarty-pants," said Sandy. "Her honey! Which the hive isn't producing much of these days. To put it bluntly, the hive is quite depressed."

"Why? It's only the most exciting and thrilling place on Earth!"

"It used to be," said Sandy. "Now it's the most monotonous place on Earth."

"Monoton-who?" said the crawdad.

"It means 'over and over and over again,'" said Herbert.

"Herbert!" declared Sandy. "You are exactly what our hive needs! With your honey recipes our hive will thrive again. Don't you see?"

"And who is going to convince the Queen?"

"YOU!" said the crawdad, aiming his monster claw at Herbert.

"And I will be there for support," said Sandy.

"Or to catch my head," said Herbert, beginning to chuckle.

"Well, what do you say?" said Sandy.

Herbert's heart began warming again. Maybe the Queen would change her mind, but how was he going to convince her to taste his honey? She may have the drones kick him out before he even has a chance to speak. But what other choice did he have? He could live down by the river for the rest of his life and keep the crawdad company, but as thrilling as that sounded (not really) nothing compared with a new chance at making the hive his home. And if it didn't work this time, he would cease making honey and build a rocket ship to launch himself into the nearest black hole.

"Fine," said Herbert.

Sandy clapped her hands and jumped up and down, while the crawdad clicked his claws.

Chapter 15

A Muddy Tribute

Sandy camped out with Herbert that evening, and the crawdad vowed to keep them both safe from frogs. This time, Herbert was more grateful for the protection.

When they woke the next morning, the sun was just peeking above the horizon. Herbert heard the raking sound coming from behind the rock again.

"What's that?" said Sandy, half awake.

Herbert crept up the side of the rock to take a peek.

"Holy honeysuckles!" Herbert yelled.

"What? What?" Sandy yelled back, making her way to Herbert.

They both stared at the crawdad putting his finishing touches on his masterpiece.

"How did you… When did you…" Herbert started.

"Sculpt that?" Sandy finished.

"It's my hobby," said the crawdad.

Herbert's jaw had nearly hit the ground. What stood before him was a heroic and gallant mud sculpture of none other than himself, although it was at least a hundred times his actual size.

"It's me," said Herbert.

"Correct," said the crawdad.

"You look so….heroic," said Sandy.

"Just a glimpse of the future, I guess," said the crawdad.

"What do you mean?" asked Herbert.

"Just a feeling you give me," said the crawdad. "After all, that's what an artist does – interpret feelings."

Herbert looked at the sculpture a bit more closely. His likeness was standing proud and tall, with a honey pail in one hand and another propped proudly against his thorax. A slight grin rested upon his face, reminding Herbert of a painting called the Mona Lisa he had seen in a magazine.

"You're unbelievably talented," said Herbert to the crawdad.

"Indeed!" said Sandy.

"We all have a purpose," said the crawdad. "Yours happens to be honey, mine happens to be mud."

Sandy stared at the ground. "I don't think I have a purpose," she said.

"Sure you do," said the crawdad.

"If only I had a chance to use it," said Sandy, her voice sounding suddenly sad.

"What do you mean?" said Herbert.

"I'm a flower scout, but the queen won't let us venture further than the clover field."

"You're kidding?" said Herbert. "No wonder the hive is depressed."

"Yep, but Her Majesty calls the shots," said Sandy.

"That's plain silly," said Herbert. "We need to speak to her immediately."

The crawdad began laughing. "I'm glad something lit your fire," he said.

"My fire was lit a long time ago," said Herbert. "It was simply beginning to burn out. But not anymore!" Herbert stood on the rock with his head up high – a perfect likeness of the sculpture before him.

"Mr. Crawdad, thank you for everything!" said Herbert. "Sandy and I have a meeting with Her Majesty the Queen Bee!"

Chapter 16

All Hail the Queen … Again

"Back for more?" said Octvious.

"He's with me," said Sandy.

"Aw, how cute," said Beauregard. "Sandy has a crush on a carcass swarmer."

"We're friends," said Herbert defensively. "And we're here to see the Queen."

"Without escorts," Sandy added.

"Suit yourselves," said Octavious. "Although you may need us after all."

"Yeah, to roll your dead bodies out of the hive when the Queen sees it's you again," said Beauregard, pointing his spear at Herbert.

"You'll thank us later," said Sandy.

"You hear that, Octavious?" said Bearegard. "We'll be thanking them later!"

The two guards doubled over in laughter. Herbert and Sandy took this opportunity to slip into the hive.

Larger and grander than Herbert remembered, the hive was truly a palace. Contained within the wooden walls of the sycamore rose honeycomb towers the size of ten banana peels. Since he wasn't being hauled to the queen by drones this time, Herbert stopped and stared as workers rushed here and there, doing their various jobs.

"Pretty amazing huh?" said Sandy.

Speechless, Herbert just hovered with his mouth gaping.

"Too bad the towers are empty," said Sandy.

"You're absolutely right," said Herbert, snapping from his trance. "How will you make it through the winter with no honey?"

"We won't."

"Yes, you will…I mean, we will!" Herbert declared. "To the Queen! Immediately!"

Sandy followed Herbert all the way to the Queen's chambers. Upon entering, Herbert felt his stomach drop to the floor.

"Did you bring the honey?" Herbert whispered briskly.

To Herbert's great relief, Sandy handed him his pail.

"My vision must be failing me!" boomed Her Majesty the Queen Bee. She pounded her scepter to the ground, which rumbled the entire hive.

Sandy shuddered and stepped back.

Herbert stepped forward.

"Your vision is perfect as ever," said Herbert.

"Then ignorance exudes from you," said the Queen. "And what bee of mine would have the gall to mingle with a garbage collector?"

"That's just it, your majesty," Sandy began.

"That wasn't a question!" said the Queen. "I should have you both exterminated."

Herbert was desperate.

"I can explain," said Herbert.

"I've heard enough explaining!" said the Queen. "As I told you before, I will not have a disgusting maggot breeder contaminating my hive! And who knows what damage you've already done. As for you, fine lady, whatever your name is-"

"Sandy, one of your flower scouts," said Sandy.

"You both deserve death, nothing less, nothing more," declared the queen. "No one disrupts the cycle of MY hive!"

"Just give me a chance," said Herbert. "I'll do anything. I'll…"

"GUARDS!" the Queen boomed.

"You're making a big mistake," said Sandy. "Herbert can save our hive from extinction."

"GUARDS!" the Queen roared louder.

"His honey recipes go beyond compare…"

While Sandy made her desperate attempts at saving their lives, Herbert resorted to a desperate action of his own. He popped the lid from his honey pail, dipped his whole hand inside, and grabbed a gooey glob of his masterpiece. Without thinking twice, Herbert launched the glob of honey squarely into the Queen's face. SPLAT!

The guards assembled around the activity and stared with what seemed to be disbelief. Time stood still except for the honey oozing down the Queen's cheeks and chin. Then, she opened her mouth, revealing her tongue, which slowly outlined her chops. Several times she began to say something but would stop and lick her lips.

"Brilliance! Sublime magnificence! Utter genius!" the Queen finally spoke. "Why didn't you let me taste the darned honey in the first place?"

"Well, uh…" Herbert began.

"We tried to…" said Sandy.

"You're hired!" declared Her Majesty the Queen Bee.

Herbert fainted.

Chapter 17

Company of the Queen

"I want to hear everything," said the Queen.

Herbert was still dizzy from hitting his head on the ground.

"Tell her how you can save the hive," Sandy said, nudging Herbert in the side.

"Your bees are bored," said Herbert. This came out quite quickly. If he had been completely conscious, Herbert would have been a bit more diplomatic.

"Bored?" said the Queen.

Herbert looked at Sandy and they both nodded.

"What should I make them do – gymnastics?" said the Queen.

"We need to build the hive's morale," said Herbert. "They are tired of doing the same old thing day after day. They need inspiration. They need energized."

"And exactly how will I do that?"

"The honey you tasted is not made from clover," Herbert urged.

"No, no, no!" said the Queen. "It is too dangerous to fly beyond the meadow. Who knows what is out there."

"I do," said Herbert.

Sandy nodded. "He has flown all the way from a d-"

"Hogsville," Herbert interrupted. He did not want Sandy to say the "D" word in front of the Queen. She barely accepted him already, let alone if she found out he had been born in a D-U-M-P.

"That does sound quite far," said the Queen. "But I'm hardly convinced to compromise my bees' safety just because you have made it this far alive."

"If you don't let your flower scouts…um…scout, then your hive won't produce enough honey to make it through the winter."

The Queen paused and thought a moment and changed the subject. "So, tell me the secret," she said. "How did you create such a remarkable honey recipe?"

"According to my experience," said Herbert. "Every flower's nectar has its own unique taste. When you pair one with another in a very precise way, you get a more flavorful honey."

"I see," said the Queen. "But what makes it so sweet."

"I sing to it," said Herbert.

"You what?" said the Queen.

Sandy looked puzzled as well.

Herbert explained the tomato article he had found (leaving out where he had found it), and the Queen seemed open to the idea.

"We do dance," said the Queen.

"I've noticed," said Herbert. "Quite well, actually."

"Well, I don't see any harm in singing while dancing," said the Queen.

"It would certainly break the monotony in the hive," said Sandy.

"Mono – what?" said the Queen.

"It will break the boredom, but that doesn't solve the remaining problem," Herbert urged again.

"Sandy," said the Queen, raising her scepter and touching it on both sides of Sandy's shoulders. "I deem you Lead Flower Scout. Take your team wherever your proboscis leads you."

Sandy's eyes widened to the size of buttercups.

"Does that solve the remaining problem?" said the Queen to Herbert.

"Why, yes, it certainly does, Your Majesty!"

"So bee it, then."

"So bee it!" Herbert and Sandy repeated.

"But first we must meet with the rest of the hive," said the Queen.

Chapter 18

The Great Bee Convention

The Queen called for a swarm in the upper branches of the sycamore tree.

"Surely she doesn't expect me to talk to the whole hive," said Herbert, noticing the thousands of bees clinging to each other and the branches.

"Well, if she does," said Sandy. "I hope you don't faint this time."

"Me too," said Herbert.

Escorted by her drones, the Queen lit on a branch and cleared her throat. The hive silenced immediately.

"I have assembled the hive today to make a special announcement," the Queen began. "As you all know, honey production is down, and at this rate we'll certainly die come winter."

A low murmur echoed through the masses.

"I have a confession to make," said the Queen. "It has been my hope to keep my hive safe by not allowing further exploration past the clover field. After all, we know the dangers of the clover field but not of the vastness beyond."

The crowd listened intently as the Queen continued.

"This has been a mistake," said the Queen. "In trying to keep you safe, I have denied you your livelihood. With clover alone, our hive has become dull, and because of that, we lack the desire and energy to keep up with the pace of years before. But…a solution has been presented to me, a solution that I never could have thought of alone."

The bees waited in quiet anticipation.

"Herbert!" summoned the Queen.

Herbert flew forward and hovered before the swarm.

"Please meet honey specialist extraordinaire, my new Chief of Staff, HERBERT THE FABULOUS!"

Unfortunately, the hive wasn't as thrilled as the Queen. Herbert barely received applause.

"Herbert, tell them your plan," said the Queen.

The silent hive made Herbert's head spin. He knew what they were thinking. Even though he had convinced the Queen, the hive still saw him only as an intruding fly. Trying several times to begin his speech, Herbert's tongue tied itself in knots. He looked at Sandy. She nodded and mouthed, go on.

"What do you know about honey that we don't," shouted a worker bee.

"Yeah," said another.

"Boo!" yelled Beauregard.

Beauregard shouldn't have done that within arm's reach of the Queen, for with one wallop of her scepter, she sent him flipping through the air.

"SILENCE!" she boomed.

The bees followed her orders but faced Herbert with straight faces.

"I know what you are thinking, and I know what you want to do to me," said Herbert. "Because if a bee entered the du- I mean the not so lovely place that I'm from, the flies would chase you away! But that is precisely why I left. I'm not like them. I never will be. I'm a fly that makes honey! It's quite simple, really."

Again, the bees murmured amongst themselves.

"But one of the perks of being an outcast is that you get to spend most of your time alone, and I spent mine perfecting my honey recipes, one of which your queen has tasted."

Sandy held up the honey pail and began passing out small samples to the crowd. Amazingly, the bees were able to divide these samples into even smaller samples to spread to more bees. Herbert watched as the bees sniffed the samples with skepticism.

"Taste it!" ordered the Queen.

As the bees nibbled their honey, Herbert hoped for the best. When the swarm began to buzz louder, Herbert wondered if they were going to praise him or chase him back to the river, but suddenly the swarm quieted again and parted in the middle. The oldest bee Herbert had ever seen made her way to the front. She sputtered when she flew, due to minor kink in her wing.

"Who is that?" said Sandy.

"She has been here much longer than me," said the Queen.

The elder bee flew towards Herbert and put out one hand to shake his. She turned around to face the swarm.

"In my days," said the elder bee. "I have never tasted such sweet and divine brilliance in honey making."

With that the elder bee flew back into the swarm, while the rest of the hive erupted in cheer.

"She's right," said a bee to Herbert's left.

"Brilliant!" said a bee to his right.

"But he is still a fly!" yelled another bee front and center. It was Octavius, and the swarm quieted to listen. "How do we know he didn't steal that honey from another hive?"

Herbert pulled a scroll made from paper bags out of his satchel and released the bottom to let it roll.

"Because I have the recipes to prove it!" shouted Herbert.

"SO, LET'S BEE-GIN!" boomed the Queen.

With a huff, Octavius flew off.

Chapter 19

The Honeycomb Chorus

Herbert was in the center of a group of bees back inside the hive.

"We have to what?" said a very confused worker bee.

"Sing to it," said Herbert. "That's the secret, seriously."

"Oh, just do as the boy says," said the elder bee from earlier. "He obviously knows what he is talking about."

"Can we dance, too?" said another worker bee. She was clearly excited.

"Of course," said Herbert.

"May I just ask why?" said the confused bee. "I mean, I'll do it. I just think it would work better if we knew why we are singing to honey."

"Positive vibrations will make it sweeter," said Herbert. "I read an article about it in a magazine, except it was for tomatoes. But I tried it with my honey and it worked."

"Can we sing whatever song we like?" asked the elder bee.

"As long as it is happy," said Herbert. "But I'll teach you my song if you want."

"Sure," said the elder bee. The others gathered closer to listen.

> *Sweet sweet nectar, O'so pure*
> *Collected from Mother Nature*
> *Give it a week and soon you'll be*
> *The sweetest most fabulous honey*

"Has a nice rhyme to it," said the elder bee. "I like it."

"How about this one," said the excited bee.

> *You make me shake!*
> *You make me prance!*
> *When I taste ya, I wanna dance!*
> *Who needs cake!*
> *Who needs pie!*
> *Nectar, Baby! I don't lie!*
> *It's so sweet!*
> *It's the best!*
> *Honey! Honey! Full of zest!*

"I love it," said Herbert.

"I've got one," said the elder bee.

> *Everybody gather' round*
> *Get ready for a funky sound*
> *This old granny's got a beat*
> *To make you wanna stomp your feet*
> *Honey! Honey! That's our fame!*
> *Sweeter! Sweeter! That's our game!*

"I'm thoroughly impressed," said Herbert. "With jingles like that – our honey has no choice but to be sweet."

"Hip-hip-hooray!" cheered the bees.

"Sounds like you guys have been busy!" said Sandy, joining the huddle.

"They sound great, don't they?" said Herbert. "Now, it is your job to teach the rest of the bees your songs. Of course they can make up songs too, but just remember – the more singing, the sweeter the honey!"

"Got it."

"Got it."

"Got it," said the bees and they each turned in a different direction to start spreading their tunes.

"I've organized our first expedition," said Sandy with a nod of seriousness. "We will go to the banks of the river and collect honeysuckle nectar."

"That will pair perfectly with the clover nectar already gathered," said Herbert.

"Perfect," said Sandy. "The flower scouts are waiting by the exit. Will you come with us?"

"I'd bee honored," said Herbert with a salute.

Chapter 20

Where the Honeysuckles Are

"Why are you being so quiet?" Sandy asked Herbert on the way to the river. "Deep in thought?"

"I just can't believe I am actually working for the beehive," said Herbert, peeking back to make sure the other flower scouts were not listening in on their conversation. "It's been my dream all my life, and here I am with you and a team of bees searching for honeysuckle nectar."

"Beats the dump, huh?" said Sandy.

"To put it lightly," said Herbert. "But to be honest – it just doesn't seem real yet. I still feel like I'm dreaming and about to be pinched any minute to wake up."

"I'll pinch you if I need to," said Sandy. "But I promise you will still be flying right next to me after you scream 'ouch.'"

Herbert nodded and sniffed the air. He could smell the fresh river water close by, which reminded him of the last time he had flown this path: he had just been rejected by the Queen.

"So, do you really think the Queen is ready to have a fly in her hive, or is she just desperate?"

"Maybe a bit of both," said Sandy. "But desperation can be a blessing and a door to opportunity… I mean, you were obviously desperate to leave everything behind and try your luck here at the hive."

"True," said Herbert.

"And you made it," said Sandy. "Just by being yourself. Sure you are a fly, but you're Herbert first."

"That's you!" said a flower scout.

The mud sculpture that the crawdad had made loomed before them.

"Jumping Junipers," said another flower scout.

"You must be famous everywhere," said another.

Herbert couldn't help but puff his chest a bit and smile at his likeness.

"Well, look who it is," said Mr. Crawdad, crawling around from behind the mud sculpture.

The flower scouts, except for Herbert and Sandy, reared their stingers.

"Put those away," said Sandy. "He's our friend."

"And I'm sorry to break it to ya," said Mr. Crawdad. "Your stingers wouldn't make it through my tough shell if you tried all day."

Tough shell, Herbert thought and giggled. It wasn't very long ago that he had been slumped over by that rock ready to give his life to some frog that hopped by.

"Oh, I was hoping we would run into you," said Sandy.

"And what a pleasant surprise," said Mr. Crawdad. "I see someone won over the Queen's heart."

"You could say that," said Sandy.

"She did make me her official Chief of Staff," said Herbert. "And Sandy is the lead flower scout!"

"Get outa town!" said Mr. Crawdad.

"Seriously!" said Herebrt.

"See, Sandy," said Mr. Crawdad. "You've found your purpose."

"I've always known my purpose. I was just never allowed to do it," said Sandy.

"All the better, then," said Mr. Crawdad.

"And here is our troop of flower scouts," said Sandy.

"Pleasure to meet you," said Mr. Crawdad.

The flower scouts nodded and said similar greetings to the crawdad.

"But what brings you back to these parts, anyway?" said the crawdad.

"Honeysuckles," said Sandy. "I could smell them last time I was here, so I know they are around somewhere."

"Right around the bend," said Mr. Crawdad.

"You're always ready to help," said Herbert. "Thank you for everything!"

"I aim to please," said Mr. Crawdad, chuckling.

Herbert, Sandy and the flower scouts said their goodbyes and buzzed off down the river. And just like the crawdad had said, the honeysuckles were right around the bend. The sweet scent blossomed all around them.

"Just look at them," said Sandy.

The honeysuckle vines grew thick along the water's edge.

"And they smell delicious," said Herbert.

"Get as much nectar as you can hold," Sandy directed the scouts.

Everyone dashed off to forage through the blossoms. When Herbert reached his first honeysuckle vine, he was overwhelmed with memories. The first flower he had ever smelled had been a honeysuckle. They grew at the edge of the dump, and he had taken some of the nectar to his mother back at the moldy banana peel. His mother loved it; his father grounded him for a week.

Now, Herbert sucked the sweet nectar from the blossom and stored it in his stomach. But as hard as he tried, he couldn't stop thinking of his mother.

Chapter 21

A Joyful Noise

When Herbert, Sandy and the flower scouts returned to the sycamore tree, they could hear the entire hive bee-bopping with song and dance. And when they entered the hive, the queen was sitting on her perch watching the show. Bees were square dancing and tap dancing. Others waltzed or tangoed, while even more were simply bobbing around, singing their hearts out.

The flower scouts immediately began spreading the word where to find the vast amounts of honeysuckles, and within seconds hundreds of bees went off to gather more nectar. Amazingly, the dancing and singing continued at full throttle, even though such a number of bees had left.

The Queen motioned with her scepter for them to come hither, and Herbert and Sandy followed the order.

"I must say," said the Queen. "I've never seen my hive so happy, and even if this song and dance method does not make the honey sweeter – at least you have brought joy to my bees. I want to thank you!"

"The gratitude is all mine," said Herbert. "And I can assure you that the honey will certainly be sweeter, and the honeysuckle nectar we're collecting is simply divine."

"Good. Good," said the Queen. "So, Sandy proves to be an excellent leader then?"

"Definitely," said Herbert.

"Thank you," said Sandy. "We're planning our next scouting before sundown."

"And what will it be this time?" said the Queen.

"I believe there are some blackberry bushes on the edge of the forest," said Sandy.

"Blackberry blossoms make excellent honey," said Herbert. "Tastes very similar to the berry itself."

"Perfect," said the Queen."

Herbert was surprised at how much freedom he and Sandy were given to develop the honey collection. The Queen really seemed to trust him, and luckily this trust paid off.

***

The days turned to weeks and soon the honeycomb palace was filled with the sweetest, most glorious honey the hive had ever known. Surprisingly, Herbert's honey recipes actually tasted sweeter than they did when he had made them alone. It must have been the added positive vibrations from the worker bees.

When the Queen called for another swarm in the sycamore's branches, Herbert wondered why. He had read that sometimes Queens do this when they plan to leave the hive. Surely she wouldn't at such a productive and happy time.

Once the bees had clung to the branches and each other, the Queen raised her scepter to silence the crowd.

"Our hive has seen great success this season and we'll undoubtedly make it through the winter!" announced the Queen.

The bees hoorayed.

"But we must give credit where credit is due," said the Queen.

Herbert could feel his face warming.

"Herbert!" boomed the Queen. "Please fly forward."

Now, he knew his face was red.

64

"It is no question that I doubted you when you first arrived, and for that I am humbled, for you have proven yourself an extraordinary bee."

Blinking his eyes rapidly, Herbert lowered his head. Had the Queen just called him a bee?

"Without your insight, guidance, and above all else, your superior talent, our hive would have perished and I along with it. So, I see it only natural to…"

Herbert felt a rush of tingly sensations run through his body.

"Crown you King of the Honeycomb Palace!"

The swarm cheered as the Queen pulled a jeweled crown made from glistening amber honeycomb from a purple velvet bag. She placed it on top of Herbert's head.

"Hip-hip-hooray!" the swarm cheered.

"But before I step down as your leader," boomed the Queen. "I declare this day a holiday! Feast and be merry!"

"Congratulations, Herbert!" said Sandy, rushing up to greet him and the Queen.

"Thank you," said Herbert. "Never in a million years did I ever imagine this happening."

Sandy darted Herbert a smirk.

"Okay, maybe I fantasized about it, but this is unbelievable," said Herbert.

"Well, believe!" said the Queen.

"But how will I ever be able to do your job?" said Herbert. "I mean…"

"The same way you made your honey," said Sandy. "The same way you journeyed to the hive."

Herbert nodded.

"You followed your…" Sandy began.

"Heart," Herbert finished.

"Yes," said the Queen.

When Herbert, Sandy and the Queen finally made their way back inside the Sycamore tree, the rest of the hive was already singing and dancing and eating their delicious honey.

Herbert let the Queen and Sandy go ahead, and he slipped back outside. There on the barky ledge, Herbert ran into his favorite beehive companions – Beauregard and Octavius.

"Nice crown," said Beauregard, shaking a bit.

"Thanks," said Herbert.

"I suppose you are going to banish us to the swamp," said Octavius.

"Nope," said Herbert.

"You're going to have us mummified and sealed in wax," said Beauregard.

"Nope," said Herbert.

"You're going to have us tied up and hung by our stingers at the top of the sycamore tree in plain view for the birds who will pluck us one by one for a …"

"Stop! Stop. Stop," said Herbert.

The two brutes just stood there, droopy-eyed and paralyzed.

"I'm giving you the day off," said Herbert.

"NO!!!" wailed Octavius. "Anything but a day… Did you say a day off?"

"He said a day off," said Beauregard.

"That's right," said Herbert. "You better get in there before I change my mind."

The two brutes scrambled inside before Herbert could say another word, but as they left, Sandy came out.

"You sure lit a fire under their stingers," said Sandy, looking back.

"Perks of the crown," said Herbert.

"Why are you out here instead of celebrating?"

"I guess I'm still soaking it all in."

"For some reason, I don't quite believe that."

"Well, I'm the king," said Herbert. "You have to believe everything I say now."

"So, this is how it's going to be?"

Herbert allowed a larger smile to spread over his face.

"I think you are homesick," said Sandy. "There it is, out in the open."

"Maybe," said Herbert.

"That's tough," said Sandy.

"Because, now, I can't go back even if I wanted to."

"Sure you can. That's the perk of having a King and a Queen – she can fill in for you while you are gone. I mean, you will have to come back."

"Definitely – I can only handle my family in small doses, except for my mother of course. I really miss my Mom."

As those words left Herbert's mouth, a scream echoed from across the meadow. Herbert recognized the voice immediately.

"Mom." Herbert whispered.

"MOM!" Herbert yelled.

Chapter 22

Trouble

Leaving Sandy behind, Herbert dashed from the sycamore tree faster than he had ever flown in his life. He quickly realized the swamp was the direction he was headed, and he hoped that what he thought was happening actually was not.

Zooming over the cattails and skimming the swamp water, Herbert found that his worst nightmare was coming true. There on a lily pad, his entire family was in the clutch of a throng of DRAGONFLIES. And the beasts were not asleep!

"Let my family go!" demanded Herbert.

"Look," said the dragonfly gripping Buford. "A Queen."

"King!" Herbert retorted, pushing the crown tighter on his head.

"Dessert, if you ask me," said the dragonfly gripping Otis.

"Fly away, Herbert," said his mother. "While you still can!"

"I won't let them eat you!" Herbert yelled.

"Good luck," said the dragonfly gripping Herbert's father.

Herbert realized that the only dragonfly that hadn't talked was the one gripping his mother. It had a crazy look in its eyes and was slobbering with drool. The only sounds coming from its mouth were gurgled chuckles.

"I said, let my family go!" Herbert shouted again.

The dragonflies ignored Herbert and the one gripping Otis placed his mouth right over Otis's head.

Herbert rushed forward. He didn't know what he could do to make the dragonfly stop, but he had to think of something before his brother lost his head.

Just then, the swamp water began to ripple and vibrate. The lily pads washed back and forth. A dark shadow moved over, bringing with it a sound of a thousand swarming, angry … BEES!

The dragonflies looked up.

Herbert looked up.

Rearing their stingers, the swarm loomed over Herbert and the carnivorous beasts below.

"I will say it one more time," shouted Herbert. "LET…MY…FAMILY…GO!"

"Or you'll each have so many stingers stuck through your hideous bodies you will wish you had been born porcupines," boomed the Queen.

The swarm lowered, inching themselves closer and closer to the four dragonflies clutching Herbert's captured family.

"I will count to THREE," said Herbert. "One…Two…"

No need counting past two. The dragonflies dropped his family on the lily pad and buzzed off into the distance with their tails between their legs.

Before Herbert could even process what had occurred, his mother had flown to him and wrapped him in a hug. She kissed his face all over.

"Oh, Herbert," she said. "I am so sorry."

"Why are you sorry, Mom?" said Herbert. "I'm the one who left, causing all of this trouble. You were almost eaten. I would have never forgiven myself."

"No. No," she said, waving at the rest of Herbert's family to join them. "It is our fault. That's why we came to find you."

"Son, I … I … I was wrong," said Herbert's father. "I was trying to make you into someone you're not. I understand that now. I feel horrible that it took you leaving the family for me to realize it, and

I'm sorry.

"It's okay, Dad," said Herbert.

"Buford! Otis!" said Herbert's mother, motioning them to join.

"Sorry, Bro!" said Otis.

"Me too," said Buford. "Will you come home now?"

Herbert looked up at the Queen and the rest of the hive still swarming in the sky. The Queen and Sandy had their hands clasped together.

"I would love to come," said Herbert. "But I've made a life for myself here. I have found somewhere that I truly belong."

The Queen nodded.

"Oh, but you belong with us," said Herbert's father.

But his mother smiled softly and shook her head.

"I will come and visit," said Herbert. "But I don't belong at the dump."

Herbert realized he had just said the "D" word in front of the Queen, but she didn't even flinch.

"You're the king, aren't you?" said his mother.

"Yes," said Herbert. "And I have a job to do."

"I am so proud of you," she said.

"Me too," said his father. "Our little maggot has become a king."

Buford and Otis bowed to their brother.

Sandy flew down from her position next to the Queen. "Would you like to take a tour of the hive while you're here?"

Herbert's father's eyes got big, and his face straightened – so did Herbert's brothers. Herbert's mother nudged her husband in the abdomen.

"We would love too," said Herbert's mother.

The Queen flew over to introduce herself. "I must say," she said. "Your son saved our hive. Without his expertise and innovation in honey making, we would have starved through winter. We owe him our lives, hence why he is King. We would be honored to have you, Herbert's own family, to celebrate his accomplishments with us at the Honeycomb Palace."

"The honor is ours," said Herbert's father.

"But do we have to eat anything?" said Buford.

"Of course," said Herbert. "Just a few small samples of every recipe I've ever made."

Buford and Otis swallowed hard, and their faces turned a pale green.

"Just kidding," said Herbert.

The relief on his brothers' faces was priceless.

"Come on," said Herbert. "I'll show you around."

Chapter 23

The King's Quarters

"You wouldn't happen to have a gas mask, would you?" asked Buford.

"Suck it up," said his mother. "A little honey never hurt anyone."

The swarm of bees swirled back into the sycamore tree and picked up the celebration where they had left off. Herbert and his family followed.

"Gorgeous!" said Herbert's mother. "I've never seen anything like it!"

"A bit high maintenance don't you think?" Herbert's father said but received a quick elbow to the side from Herbert's mother.

"I mean … fancy," he tried again. "Nice and fancy."

"We'll let the five of you alone," said the Queen, grabbing Sandy's hand. "But, Herbert, I suggest you show them your throne."

"Throne?" said Otis.

Herbert smiled. "Yep."

"Way cool," said Buford.

Herbert led his family up through the towers of honeycomb to The King's Quarters. When they reached the throne room, Herbert gazed at the magnificence before him. The throne was easily twenty times his size with glistening jewels of amber honey adorning it from top to bottom. How will I sit in that thing? Herbert thought. But it would be a while before he found out.

"Do you mind if I sit in it?" said Otis.

"Me, too. Me, too," said Buford.

"Where are your manners?" said Herbert's mother.

"I wouldn't mind taking a turn myself," said Herbert's father.

Herbert didn't know whether to laugh or cry. His family was enjoying themselves in a beehive.

"Well, maybe we could all take a turn," said Herbert's mother. "If Herbert says it's okay."

"Of course," Herbert shouted. "My treat."

Herbert watched as his family took turns sitting on his throne and acting as King or Queen. And as he watched, he felt the happiest he had ever felt. It took Herbert a second to realize why, but then it chimed. For the first time, Herbert felt not only that he was a part of his family, but that they were a part of him.

"Okay, Herbert," said his mother. "It is all yours."

Herbert flew to his throne and took a seat. Surprisingly, he didn't feel any different sitting in that big chair than he had all summer working at the hive. Then he remembered what Sandy had said. "You are Herbert first." And he still was. It didn't matter what title he was given: fly, bee, or even king. Herbert was still Herbert, and he always would BEE.

THE AUTHOR

Professor Watermelon (Chadwick Gillenwater) travels the country inspiring elementary students to use the written word as a joyful way of creative self-expression. As an experienced school librarian, storyteller and children's author, Professor Watermelon has the tools to motivate his students to build characters, twist plots, and dream-up new worlds. To learn more about Professor Watermelon and his creative writing classes, take a look at his blog: www.professorwatermelon.com

THE ILLUSTRATOR

Josh Smart resides in Indianapolis, Indiana where he is the resident cartoonist for the Indiana Pacers. He has also provided cartoons and illustrations for other NBA and NFL teams as well as Pepsi, Kroger and the American Red Cross. Illustrating children's books is Josh's passion, and he looks forward to creating many more books with Professor Watermelon. You can reach Josh at smartoonist@gmail.com

Made in the USA
Charleston, SC
19 January 2013